A Treasury of
Children's
CLASSICS

Commissioning Editor   Christine Deverell
Additional Illustrations   Richard Deverell
Design   Ian Jones

©2000 Robert Frederick Limited
4-5 North Parade
Bath, U.K.
BA1 1LF

Printed in China

A Treasury of
Children's
CLASSICS

THREE FAIRY TALES
Adapted by
CHRISTINE DEVERELL

· C O N T E N T S ·

Beauty and the Beast

ILLUSTRATED BY DAVID LONG

Once upon a time there was a merchant who had three beautiful daughters. The eldest sisters cared only for fine dresses and jewels, but the youngest, called Beauty, had a kind and gentle heart, and was especially loved by her father. One day, the merchant was going off on a long journey, and he asked his daughters what they would like him to bring home. "I'd like a fine, emerald necklace," said the eldest. "And a pearl necklace for me," cried the second. "I would like you to bring yourself home as soon as possible," said Beauty, "and if you can find one, I would like a white rose."

The two sisters made fun of Beauty for asking their father to bring her a rose. "You have lots of roses in your garden," they said. "But I do not have a white one," said Beauty, and she wondered why they wanted jewels. The merchant did not forget his daughters' wishes, and before returning home he bought an emerald necklace and a pearl necklace.

But nowhere could he find a white rose for Beauty, for it was winter, and snow was falling. As he was nearing home, the merchant missed his way in the snowstorm, and could not tell where he was. Just as he was about to turn round, he saw lights ahead, and soon found himself at the door of a great castle.

10

He hoped that they would offer him shelter for the night, and as he went to knock on the door, he saw that it was open.

Not a servant was in sight, so he went inside. In the great hall, he found a splendid supper laid out. He sat down and enjoyed the feast. In the corner of the hall was an open door, and when he looked in, he saw a bedroom that looked as if it had been prepared for him.

The merchant was very tired, so he went to bed and slept soundly. In the morning a fine suit had been laid out for him to wear, and a hearty breakfast awaited him in the hall. He would have liked to thank his kind host, but still the merchant saw no one. As he walked through the garden on his way to the stable to collect his horse, he spied a beautiful rose bush covered with white blooms.

Thinking of his daughter and her request, he reached out and picked a single rose. Suddenly a terrible roar sounded from the bushes and a huge, ugly beast sprang out.

"Who is stealing my white rose?" he growled. The poor merchant trembled and could barely speak. "I did not mean to steal.

"My daughter begged me to bring her a white rose and this

is the only one I have seen." "It is my favourite rose, and anyone who touches it must die!" said the Beast, "But I will let you go if you promise to bring me the first thing that runs to meet you when you get home." The merchant agreed, and as he made his journey home, he hoped that it might be the cat that came out to meet him, and not his beloved dog.

But as he approached the house, it was his little daughter Beauty who came running towards him. He turned so pale that when she saw her father, Beauty thought he must be very sick. He gave her the white rose and took her hand. He told her all that had happened to him and the promise he had made to the Beast. "But I will never,  never give you up Beauty," he said. "You must keep your promise, Father," said Beauty, "perhaps he will not hurt me."

So they prepared to return to the castle. They rode silently through the forest, for they were too sad to speak. At the castle they found the front door open and a meal laid out in the great hall, only this time the table was set for two. They sat down, but Beauty and her father could not eat. Then, at nine o'clock, they heard a great roar and the Beast appeared.

He spoke gently to them, saying to the merchant, "You may stay here tonight, but tomorrow you must go home and leave Beauty behind. Do not worry about her; she will have all she could wish for here." Father and daughter parted with great sadness. But Beauty soon became quite contented with her life in the castle. Her room was very pretty, with roses outside her window, and on a table stood a wonderful mirror. In golden letters around the outside was written, "See your wishes, here enshrined, What you long for, you will find."

"I will be able to wish myself home whenever I am unhappy," said Beauty to herself. And she often looked into the mirror to see what was happening to her father and sisters at home, for she spent every day amusing herself, and saw no one until the evening when the Beast joined her for supper. After they had eaten Beauty would sing to the Beast. One night he asked her, "Do you think I am very ugly?" His voice sounded so sad that Beauty found it hard to answer him. "You have a very kind face," she said at last with a sigh, "but you really are very ugly."

15

A single tear ran down the Beast's cheek, and Beauty felt so sorry for him. "I do like you very much," she assured him. "Then will you marry me, Beauty?" "O, no! I could never marry a beast," sobbed Beauty. She went to bed very sad, and looking into the magic mirror she asked to see her family again. The mirror painted a picture of her old home, and in the corner Beauty saw her dear father lying ill in bed.

Next day Beauty could neither play nor work, and could only wait until supper-time came when she could ask the Beast if he would let her go home for just one week to visit her father." If you go you will never come back to me," said the Beast. "I promise you I will come back in a week, dear Beast. Let me go," pleaded Beauty. "Very well," he said, "but take this ring with you, and if you ever want to come back, put it on your finger when you go to bed, and in the morning you will find yourself here in your own room."

17

That night Beauty looked into the magic mirror and wished herself home. She fell asleep on her bed tightly clutching the ring, and when she woke she was in her father's house. He wept with joy to see his little Beauty again, and began to get well. At the end of one week, Beauty could not bear to leave her father, so she broke her promise to the Beast and stayed another week.

One night, she had a strange dream. She dreamed that she was back in the Beast's garden, wandering about. As she came to the white rose bush she found the poor Beast lying on the ground, and he looked as if he were dying. As she ran towards him he cried out, "Oh Beauty, you have broken my heart, and I shall die without you." Beauty woke up from her dream and so longed to see her dear Beast again that she reached out for the magic ring and slipped it onto her finger.

When she next awoke, she found herself back in her pretty room in the Beast's castle, just as he had told her she would. Remembering her dream, Beauty quickly ran out into the garden to see if he was there. When she reached the white rose bush she found the Beast lying so stiff and quiet that she thought he was dead.

18

"Oh my dear Beast," cried Beauty as she threw her arms
around his neck. "Please don't die, for I have come back to take
care of you, and I will marry you, for I love you with all my
heart." She put her head in her hands and wept, and when she
stood up, she could not see the Beast. Instead, through the tears,
she could only see a handsome young Prince beside her. "Who are
you? And what have you done with my Beast?" asked Beauty.

"Do you not know me, dear Beauty?" said the Prince. "I am
the Beast you loved and to whom you gave life and happiness. A

witch cast an evil spell over me so that I took the form of an ugly beast, and nothing could set me free until a beautiful girl loved me and promised to marry me." "If you really are my dear Beast, then I will marry you," said Beauty. Together they went to the magic mirror, and when Beauty looked in she saw her father living for the rest of his days in the castle with her. When the Prince looked in the mirror he saw a wedding, with Beauty his bride carrying a bouquet of white roses. Their wishes came true, and they lived happily ever after.

The Ugly Duckling

ILLUSTRATED BY KEN OLIVER

It was summertime, and it was beautiful in the country. The sunshine fell warmly on an old house surrounded by deep canals. From the wall around the house to the edge of the water there grew large burdock leaves, so high that children could hide in them, and it was here that a duck had built her nest and laid her eggs. She was growing very tired of sitting on her eggs when at last she heard a crack.

One little head popped out, then another, and then another. They waddled out to the edge of the leaves and peeped out. "The world is so big!" they said to their mother.

She counted the ducklings and checked the nest, and there was one egg, the largest, that lay unhatched.

The mother duck sat on the egg until at last it cracked open, and out tumbled the largest and ugliest duckling she had ever seen. "That is a big, strong creature," she said, "not at all like the others."

The next day the sun was shining warmly when the mother duck and her family went down to the canal. Splash! she went into the water, and called to the ducklings to follow. One by one they jumped in, and they swam quite easily.

Even the ugly grey one was swimming around with the rest of them. "Quack, quack!" said the mother duck. "Come with me now, and I will show you the world; but keep close to me or someone may tread on you, and watch out for the cat." They came to the duckyard, where other duck families were gathered. "You must bow to the old duck that you see over there," said the mother duck, "for she is nobly born and of Spanish blood."

The other ducks in the yard stared at the new brood, and then began to talk to each other; "Look how ugly that one is!" they said, and one of the ducks flew at him and bit his neck. "Leave him alone," said his mother, "he is not doing any harm." "Those are fine children that you have," said the old duck, "they are all very pretty except for that one."

"Certainly, he is not handsome," said the mother, "but he is very good and he can swim as well as the others, indeed rather better." She stroked the Ugly Duckling's neck with her beak and smoothed his ruffled feathers. The day did not go well for the poor Ugly Duckling. He was bitten, pecked and teased by both ducks and hens and the turkeys terrified him.

Things got much worse as the days went by; the girl who fed the poultry kicked him, and even his own brothers and sisters were unkind to him. He decided to run away. He ran through the hedge, and the little sparrows were frightened and flew away.

"That is because I am so ugly," he thought, and ran on. He came to a moor where some wild ducks lived. "You are really very ugly,' said the wild ducks to their new companion, "but that

26

does not matter to us, as long as you do not wish to marry into our family."

Poor thing! He had no thought of marrying. All he wanted was to live among the reeds and drink the water on the moor. He was happy there for two days, but on the third day he awoke to the sound of guns and barking dogs, and the sight of ducks and geese falling from the sky.

He kept very still as the dogs splashed about in the mud, bending the reeds and rushes in all directions. For one terrifying moment, a fierce looking dog thrust his nose into the duckling's face, and then ran off.

"Well!" said he to himself, "I am so ugly that even a dog does not want to look at me."

It was late in the afternoon before silence fell, and the Ugly Duckling waited another hour before he ran away as fast as he could from the moor. As it grew dark he reached a little hut, and when he saw that the door was broken, leaving a hole big enough for him to get through, he crept inside. In this one roomed hut there lived an old woman with her cat who sat on her lap and purred contentedly, and a hen who laid good eggs.

They were all asleep and
did not notice their visitor
until the morning. The cat
mewed and the hen began to
cackle. "What's the matter?"
asked the old woman, looking
round. Her eyes were not
good, and she took the
duckling to be a fat duck who
had got lost. "If this is not a
drake, we might have duck's eggs as well as hen's eggs."

For three weeks the duckling sat in a corner of the hut
feeling very sad. One day the old woman opened the door and he
felt the bright sunshine on his feathers.

This gave him such a yearning to swim that he could not
help but tell the hen. "What is the matter with you?" said the hen.
"You have nothing to do all day, so you sit here dreaming. Why
don't you lay eggs, or purr, and forget these fantasies?" "Oh, but
it is so delicious to swim," said the duckling, "so delicious when
the waters close over your head and you plunge to the bottom."

"I think you must be crazy," said the hen, "why don't you ask the cat - he is the wisest creature I know - whether he would like to swim, or to plunge to the bottom of the water. Or ask your mistress. No one is cleverer than she. Do you think she would take pleasure in swimming, and in the waters closing over her head?"

"You do not understand me," sobbed the Ugly Duckling.

"What! do you think yourself wiser than the cat and the old woman, not to mention myself? You ought to be grateful for all the kindness that has been shown to you here. Do you not have a warm room to live in? And are you not lucky to have our company and the benefit of our wisdom and experience? Believe me, I want you to be happy. I know I tell you unpleasant truths, but this is what friends are for. Come on, do yourself a favour and learn to purr or to lay eggs."

"I think I will take my chance, and go out into the wide world again," said the duckling.

"Well, off you go then," said the hen, and he escaped through the open door. He soon found water, and swam on the surface and plunged to the bottom. But all the other animals ignored him: "It's because I am so ugly," he said to himself.

Autumn came, and the leaves turned yellow and brown. The poor little Ugly Duckling began to shiver as the air grew colder. One evening, just as the sun was setting, a flock of large birds took to the sky. They were the most beautiful creatures the duckling had ever seen; their feathers were of a white, and their necks were long and slender. They were swans, and they flew away to warmer climes.

It was a cold, cold winter, and the poor little duckling felt so alone. He very nearly froze to death in the ice, when a peasant noticed him, picked him up and took him home to his wife and children. He soon revived, and the children wanted to play with him, but he was afraid of them, and ran away into the snow again.

It would be just too sad to tell you all the things that happened to him that winter. He was lying beside the canal among some reeds one day when he felt the warmth of the sun on his feathers. The larks were singing and spring had returned. The Ugly Duckling came out into the sunshine and shook his wings. They were stronger than before, and he flew, close to the water, until he landed in a garden with apple trees in full blossom. The sights and the smells were delightful.

Three beautiful swans came swimming proudly along the canal. The duckling was so excited when he saw them that he flew into the water and swam towards them.

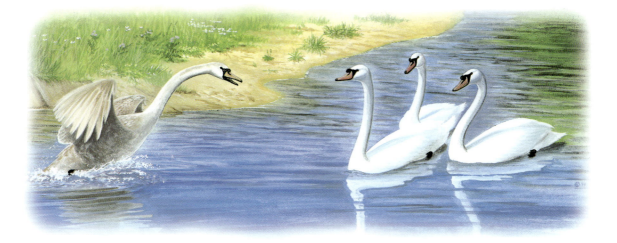

33

"They will probably ignore me, for I am so ugly," he thought, and he hung his head in shame. As he did so, he caught sight of his reflection in the water. And what he saw before him was not a plump, ugly, grey bird, but a beautiful, white swan!

The larger swans swam around him and stroked his neck with their beaks, and he was very happy.

He remembered how he had
been laughed at and
cruelly treated, and
now he heard
everyone say that
he was the most
beautiful of all
birds. He said to
himself, "How
little did I dream
of so much
happiness when I
was the ugly, despised
duckling!"

34

Goldilocks & the Three Bears

ILLUSTRATED BY RICHARD DEVERELL

There were once upon a time three bears who lived in a house in the woods. There was a Little Baby Bear, a Mother Bear and a Big Father Bear.

Each had a bowl for its porridge: a tiny bowl for the Little Baby Bear, a medium sized bowl for Mother Bear, and a great big bowl for the Big Father Bear.

Each had a chair to sit on: a tiny chair for the Little Baby Bear, a medium sized chair for Mother Bear and a great big chair for the Big Father Bear.

Each had a bed to sleep in: a tiny bed for the Little Baby Bear, a medium sized bed for Mother Bear and a great big bed for the Big Father Bear.

One day, after they had made the porridge for their breakfast, they decided to go for a walk to give the porridge time to cool down. While they were out, a little girl named Goldilocks passed the house.

She was not a good, polite little girl, and she peered through the windows and peeped through the keyhole. When she saw that no one was at home, she lifted the latch and went inside.

She saw the bowls of porridge on the breakfast table and not having eaten yet, decided to help herself. She tried the Big Father Bear's porridge, but that was too salty. Then she tried the Mother Bear's porridge, and that was too sweet. Then she tried the Little Baby Bear's porridge, and that was just right; neither too salty, nor too sweet, and she ate it all up.

39

Then Goldilocks sat down in Big Father Bear's chair. It was much too hard, so she tried Mother Bear's chair. That was much too soft. So she tried Little Baby Bear's chair, and it felt perfect. But after she had sat in Little Baby Bear's chair for just a few seconds, the leg broke, and Goldilocks crashed to the floor!

Goldilocks went upstairs, hoping to find a comfortable bed. She lay down on Big Father Bear's bed. It was much too hard, so she tried Mother Bear's bed. That was much too soft.

So she tried Little Baby Bear's bed, and it felt perfect. She got right under the covers and fell fast asleep.

While she slept, the three bears came home for their breakfast. Goldilocks had made quite a mess on the table.

"Who's been eating my porridge?" boomed Big Father Bear in his great, gruff voice. "Who's been eating my porridge?" said Mother Bear in her cross voice. "And who's been eating my porridge?" cried Little Baby Bear in his squeaky little voice, "And they've eaten it all up!"

They looked around the room and saw that the furniture had been moved. They went over to their chairs. "Who's been sitting on my chair?" boomed Big Father Bear in his great, gruff voice. For Goldilocks had used the hard cushion to wipe the porridge off her fingers. "Who's been sitting on my chair?" said Mother Bear in her cross voice. For Goldilocks had left a big dent in the soft cushion. "And who's been sitting on my chair?" cried Little Baby Bear in his squeaky little voice, "And they've broken it!" By now poor Little Baby Bear was in tears.

Together the three bears went upstairs to the bedroom. First, they came to Big Father Bear's bed. "Who's been lying on my bed?" boomed Big Father Bear in his great, gruff voice. For Goldilocks had crumpled the sheets. "Who's been lying on my

bed?" said Mother Bear in her cross voice. For Goldilocks had thrown the soft pillows onto the floor, and left a dirty mark on the fine quilt.

"And who is that sleeping in my bed?" cried Little Baby Bear in his squeaky little voice through his tears. "Look! She ate my porridge! She broke my chair! She made a mess in our house! And now, there she is! She's sleeping in my bed!"

Suddenly, Goldilocks woke up and saw the three bears staring down at her crossly. She sprung out of the bed and sped down the stairs, out of the front door and into the wood. The three bears heard Goldilocks crying out: "There's bears in the wood! Help! Help! There's bears in the wood!" Her voice faded into silence, and the three bears were never bothered by her again.